ROSIE AND THE SECRET OF THE SNOGARD

ROSIE AND THE SECRET OF THE SNOGARD

OLIVIA MERRYDALE

TRAIGH BAN

TRAIGH BAN

First published in 2023 by Traigh Ban,
Great Britain

Hardback ISBN: 978-1-7391870-3-3

eBook ISBN: 978-1-7391870-4-0

TRAIGH BAN 2023

To Marc and my parents, with love

Contents

PROLOGUE

Once upon a time there lived...

There are many different ways to start telling this story.

We could start with the dragons, wronged long ago. That approach though, might require us to immediately launch into an explanation of the whole saga of the curse, called down upon the royal house by the foolishness of the king, queen and princess themselves. Then we would already be in the nitty-gritty of our actual story and might not get around introducing (shudder), at this frightfully early stage, the Lady Rosamund...

Another approach would be to go back in time and describe the beautiful northern kingdom with its rugged coastline, its sea caves and birds, the old cursed ruin and Dragon's Point, that high-peaked island far out at sea. It would perhaps lead us to describe the charming coastal town with its half-moon harbour, but also the lovely meadows, the little woods and the huge variety of beaches. From there we could delve into its history of the childless king and queen and the story of the first dragon whisperer – so the legends have it – to be born at the castle.

We could also just start, very prosaically, with an afternoon in late spring and King Edmar, along with some members of his household, standing at the entrance to his ancestral home, waiting for the arrival of a carriage. This carriage was meant to convey his niece Rosalind, recently turned his ward, into his care. The timing wasn't good. The king was under immense pressure to find a solution to a very complicated problem and it was consequently not a good moment to have his spoilt sister's daughter foisted on him. He had briefly considered getting out of the arrangement but had concluded that to be dishonourable. He had promised the child's father a long time ago to look after any of his children, should there ever be a need for it, and he stood by this. Still, he was uneasy. In all the years that had passed between that promise and now he had never even seen his sister or his brother-in-law, let alone met his niece. Outside the king's closest circle it was not even known that the child existed and he fully intended to keep it that way. Matters were complicated enough.

The afternoon light had taken on that warm quality that gave the yellow stone of the castle's front its golden glow, when the sound of hooves became audible in the distance. A moment later the carriage, pulled by four horses, turned into the lane. It pulled up and King Edmar braced himself.

I

THE KING'S NIECE

It was later, when they were sitting in the parlour after their evening meal had finished, that King Edmar, looking sideways at his niece, really allowed himself to think of her. She was nothing like his sister; that much was certain. He had definitely been taken aback when the door to the carriage opened and a mere slip of a girl had emerged. Clutching a grubby teddy bear to her chest, her large green eyes – flecked with hazel and rimmed with grey just like her uncle's – had looked around warily. She had a mop of rather short untidy brown hair that stuck out at odds and angles and her clothes consisted of a scruffy pair of boots,

3

a loose pair of trousers and a thick jumper that was at least three sizes too big for her. It had taken a lot of delicacy and careful coaxing to get her into the house.

King Edmar was still not entirely sure what he had expected but he had certainly not been prepared for a little girl with such a very solemn and scared expression in her eyes. After the initial brief glance, she had avoided looking at him. All the way through the castle, she had trailed slightly behind him, holding her bear very tightly as if she was afraid someone might try and take him from her. That bear had certainly seen better days but there nothing wrong with him that couldn't get fixed by someone who knew their job. The king made a mental note to engage Clara, the seamstress who was known to work wonders on much-loved soft toys.

One thing that King Edmar had noticed, on several occasions during their journey through the castle and also during the meal, was that his niece's gaze seemed to, periodically, attach itself to certain objects for no immediately discernable reason. Otherwise she appeared to draw as little attention to herself as possible. King Edmar had to admit that the stuck-up princess he had expected to come from his sister's court might in some ways perhaps have been easier to deal with. It would certainly have been less concerning than this little girl, who had so clearly known neglect. He was trying to puzzle her out as unobtrusively as he could during the walk to the parlour and their subsequent meal but he was getting nowhere. He watched her pick up her teaspoon, the one with the tiny dragon wrought on the handle, and saw her startle. For a moment she seemed completely absorbed and when she looked up her eyes held an expression of wonder. The king stared at his niece, millions of thoughts and fragments racing through his mind at once before settling into place. Suddenly he was sure of at least one thing.

"I'll be right back," he said to her and left the room, hurrying down the corridor towards the far wing, wondering if his instinct could possibly be right.

Hazy morning sunlight was streaming through the mullioned windows into the room. The main part of the curtains had been drawn the night before, but one had been left open to allow moonlight to enter the room and take the shadows away. The girl lying in the four-poster bed was still fast asleep. The long journey the day before and her arrival at her uncle's castle had exhausted her. For the moment the room, and the castle with it, held its breath. There were strange disturbances in the air with a hint of possibility thrown in. It had undoubtedly taken a long time for the room's new occupant to take their place. For now the room was content to wait and see.

The blackbird, perched on the low wall of the terrace outside, had other ideas though. His early morning call broke into Rosie's slumber slowly waking her. She opened her eyes, at first utterly confused as to where she was, and then remembered the day before. Her hand reached out and closed around the comforting shape of Sir Redhill, her teddy bear. He too had had a long and strange day yesterday. Sir Redhill was probably still marvelling over his new state of cleanliness. After the meal last night, both he and Rosie had been put into a bath. But while Rosie had merely been taken to her room afterwards, Sir Redhill had been mended. Now both of his ears and his right arm were properly attached and neat again.

Rosie sat up and looked around. The room was spacious but not too large. From her four-poster bed she caught a glimpse of the sky through the large bay window to her left, which was set in honey-coloured panelling with a window seat going round its entire base, topped with a delicately floral-patterned and cream cushioning. Part of the bay window was also taken up by a small desk and a chair. The lower part of the wall opposite her was panelled too, with pretty wallpaper dotted with tiny flowers visible above. A fireplace surrounded by creamy marble was nearly exactly opposite her bed. A comfortable looking armchair was angled in front with a small round table beside it. On her right, taking up the space to the right side of the door, was a large inbuilt wardrobe. In the other corner she caught a glimpse of shelves which appeared to be empty.

Suddenly she felt wide awake. She pushed back the covers and got out of bed. Despite the fireplace being empty the room was warm. Going round the bed she spotted a chaise longue at the foot of it and sat down to pull on the clothes laid out for her there. Someone must have washed and mended the clothes she had arrived in because, apart from being ragged, they were clean. This made her feel a bit better about putting them on. Before she was packed off to her uncle's, no one in her mother's household seemed to have cared very much about anything anymore, least of all that disappointing little princess.

At the bottom of the pile she found something that didn't belong to her. It was a jumper, made from wool, and soft to the touch. Holding it up she saw that worked into the mossy-green body on the front was a picture of the sea with islands dotted around in the background. It seemed to whisper to her. For a moment she thought she heard water lapping against rock and the cry of seabirds wheeling through the sky. This was definitely not hers but it was exactly her size and she couldn't resist putting it on.

Still marvelling at its loveliness, she wandered over to the window and looked out. A way off, very tall and sweeping, stood a massive cedar tree, close to where the lawn seemed to end, opening up to a long view beyond. In the distance, more trees were dotted around in different places and further still; everything was only just beginning to emerge from the early morning mist.

Closer to the castle, on the left, was a large stone archway, set in a tall grey wall that seemed lead to a garden beyond. A plant was growing along the top of it and, on either side of the entrance, sat some large stone creatures. They almost gave her the feeling of guarding something but that was a silly idea of course. Stone couldn't move. She gazed at them a little longer and for a moment she had the weird sensation that one of those great creatures had lifted its head, very briefly, to gaze back at her. Her heart thumped loudly and she clutched Sir Redhill to her chest.

Before she had much time to puzzle this over there was a knock on her door. A very husky sort of "Yes...?" made it out of her mouth but that seemed enough, for the next moment the door was pushed open and Maria, the maid who had bathed her the night before, appeared with a large tray of food and drink.

"His Majesty sends his apologies. He had some urgent business to attend to and won't be back until the evening. He asked our cook to prepare a breakfast for you and then Mrs Baird, the housekeeper, will be taking you into town for some shopping." When Rosie only blinked confusedly, she continued, "Well, you didn't bring very many clothes." She bit her bottom lip in a worried fashion, when she noticed the blush creeping up Rosie's neck and into her cheeks.

"King Edmar said he didn't want to choose for you," Maria rushed on, anxious to overcome the sticky patch they suddenly found themselves in, "so he said it would be best if you had a look for yourself. See what you like, you know?"

Rosie stared at her in bewilderment.

"Oh my, this is coming out all wrong," Maria sighed. "The important thing to know is that Mrs Baird will be going into town with you after breakfast." Maria beamed at Rosie, who was still trying to absorb all these snippets of information. She hated shopping. But if she had to, she fervently hoped that she might be allowed to choose at least one piece that she really liked. Past expeditions with her mother though had taught her to expect very little in that way.

2

HALF-MOON BISCUITS
AND THE MURAL

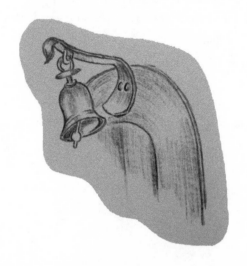

Later that morning Rosie and Mrs Baird left for town. Looking out of the carriage's window she tried to take in as much as she could: sheep and lambs, green fields, hedges with glossy green foliage, a blue sky and – on two occasions – a glimpse of the sparkling sea. The excitement of the ride made Rosie almost forget how very uncomfortable she had felt earlier that morning.

Before setting off, Mrs Baird had gone through all of Rosie's clothes and told her that "most of them will have to go, love". Her good frocks, bought long ago before her mother had lost interest in everything, were all too small for her. There wasn't even a point in trying them on. Most of the other clothes she had been given while various other people attempted to keep things together, trying to figure out what to do with her. Finally, the lawyers had unearthed a paper, in which her father had named King Edmar her guardian should anything ever befall him. After that events had moved swiftly and within a week she had been bundled off to her uncle's.

The carriage turned another corner now and a tall tower built of pale stone became visible in the distance. The road started to descend. Craning her neck, Rosie could make out a town, nestled into the hollow of the valley, and behind it the masts of ships sitting in a dazzlingly blue sea.

When they had passed through the town gates, Rosie wished her eyes could be everywhere at once. There was so much to see: people walking about in all sorts of different coloured clothes and the houses themselves looked so completely different from anything Rosie had ever seen. Up one street, as they were driving past, she even spotted a bench built around a large tree. She was itching to turn the handle and get out of the carriage but with eleven years she was old enough to know that jumping out of a carriage while driving through a busy town was not a good idea. Finally they came to a courtyard, clearly meant for waiting carriages and their horses, and set off through an arched gateway into the bustling streets beyond.

Rosie had never been in a town quite like this before. Everywhere she looked there were people buying, selling or simply looking at things. Some stood around talking and – fascinatingly – no one was paying any particular attention to either Mrs Baird or herself. At home, on the few occasions she had been allowed to accompany her mother, there had always been a path cleared for them, which her mother swept down haughtily. The people around them had bowed or at the very least inclined their heads respectfully. Usually they would end up in some place where Rosie was expected to sit still for hours on end, until her back ached and her seat began to feel very uncomfortable. If she stirred, her mother would glance at her with the expression that told Rosie that there would be no dessert that evening or servant released from duty in order to read her bedtime story unless she held still immediately.

Mrs Baird, noticing the subtle shift in pressure on her hand, looked down to see that tense expression from earlier that morning back on the child's face. It made her sad and uneasy to see the girl like this. Fortunately, before she could dwell on it too much, they reached the dressmaker's shop. For the next hour and a half they were busy sorting out Rosie's new wardrobe.

The shopping was a breeze, leaving Rosie to marvel at the novelty of it all. She got measured for a blouse and a dress with pockets, something her mother had never allowed her. Mrs Baird let her choose her own colours and she even encouraged her to try on some trousers, when she saw her lingering. "Might as well, lass, as you cannot easily climb trees in any of those," she said, pointing to the skirts and dresses. Rosie's head had reeled. They finally left the shop with several dresses and skirts, more than one pair of trousers, shirts, an additional night-dress and enough socks and underwear to stop Rosie worrying about that for a long time. Mrs Baird insisted too on a cardigan and a jacket, as the evenings could still be nippy despite it being almost summer. Finally they got a pair of shoes, some sandals and even a pair of sturdy boots with a good grip at the shoemaker's next door. While Rosie left wearing the new shoes, Mrs Baird arranged for her old pair to be re-heeled. With arrangements to have the things conveyed to the carriage, they left for town "to recover our spirits", as Mrs Baird put it.

It was on that walk through town that Rosie discovered what an excellent companion Mrs Baird was. She had never been allowed to tarry. Her mother or – in earlier years her nursemaid – had always hurried her along, told her off for loitering ('unbecoming for a princess') and would definitely not have encouraged her to enter stationery shops or toyshops or indeed any shop, that contained even the faintest thing of interest to Rosie. The cobbled streets wound on in no particular pattern. They passed through numerous narrow alleys, went down steps and climbed up little winding paths. There were benches and trees dotted around the town and squares with shops and houses off it, decorated with tubs and hanging baskets overflowing with flowers. Just when Rosie was beginning to feel exhausted, they turned into yet another little cobbled square. This one was surrounded by buildings with a wrought-iron structure arching across the entrance to it. Cottage flowers grew in the neatly kept gardens in front of the houses. When they passed through the archway, Rosie smelt the scent of delicious baking and found, to her great delight, that Mrs Baird was making straight for a small café, situated diagonally opposite the archway. The bell inside the door gave a light tinkling chime and Rosie found herself in the cosiest space she had ever been in.

There was a counter with a display of éclairs, half-moon biscuits, cakes decorated with fruits, nuts and tiny flowers and other delicacies, and shelves behind it on which loaves of bread were laid out in neat and mouth-watering rows. To the left, two steps down, in an area with a pastel-coloured floor and rich buttery yellow walls, a small number of tables and chairs were set out invitingly. In the corner, flanked either side by bookshelves, was even an armchair with a round table in front of it. At the table next to it, this one square, a slender young woman with autumn-coloured red hair sat bent over a sketch pad, her pen moving rapidly across the page in front of her.

"Good day to you Mrs Green," Rosie overheard Mrs Baird strike up a conversation with the white-haired woman behind the counter, who made Rosie think of the kind grandmothers in the fairy tales her father had sometimes told her.

Drifting away from the grown-ups' conversation Rosie suddenly caught sight of the wall at the back of the café. It was taken up almost entirely by a mural. The thing that intrigued her most about it though, was that the scene seemed familiar. It depicted the sea fringed with cliffs, a cluster of islands in the background, and flying through the air were not only gulls and large white birds with black-tipped wings but also a huge blue dragon. While she stood there Rosie had the strangest sensation of almost being drawn into the picture. She heard the sea lashing itself against the rocks below the cliff edge, heard sea birds calling out and the beating of the dragon's wings on the wind, accompanied – she could have sworn – by the sound of someone whooping with joy.

In that instance several things happened at once, too quick to say which was first. As she stood, still mesmerised, she noticed the shape of one of the islands at the very back. It was pointing, almost needle-like, into the sky but was covered all over in green vegetation. Looking down she realised that the same island and indeed the entire same group of islands were also what was depicted on her jumper. She let out a gasp of surprise. Suddenly there was a whispering coming from the mural and also from the air around her. The words were impossible to make out but they chilled her. They carried with them so much sorrow and regret. The pain contained in them was almost physical. 'It was wrong!' was the only phrase that ricocheted clearly through her mind and apparently behind her. Grasping a chair to steady herself she turned around and saw the red-haired woman stare at her, blue eyes wide, with something akin to recognition in her face.

The moment was broken by Mrs Baird bustling over with a tray.

"My poor love, you must be faint with hunger after all that shopping. I shouldn't have left you waiting for so long."

Rosie allowed herself to get steered into a comfortable chair and gratefully accepted first a glass of water and then a mug of hot chocolate. On the plate Mrs Baird put in front of her were some small biscuits shaped like half-moon crescents. Rosie took a bite out of one of them and their delicate texture with a hint of lemon and vanilla drove any musings about whispers out of her mind. She didn't dare look over to the red-haired woman again. Whatever had happened just moments before was strange, almost uncanny, and she wasn't sure if she wanted to probe it too much.

3

THE SLEEPER IN THE GARDEN

There wasn't much – when it crossed her mind a few weeks later – Rosie could recall in detail from her trip into town. So much had happened in the meantime, with her tour of the castle and grounds – disorientating due to the sheer size of the place – being just one of them. It isn't easy to settle into a new home when you are young, especially when you are on your own and expectations seem so different from everything you have known until that point.

Rosie's uncle, though very busy with various things, tried to have at least one mealtime with her each day. The first few nights he even came to her room in the evenings to ask her about her day. Sitting in the chair drawn over from the desk though, conversation would peter out. Neither uncle nor niece seemed to be naturally communicative spirits with people that they weren't familiar with and the degree of relationship did not automatically make for closeness. In the end, by some unspoken but understood mutual agreement, they left off on those talks. This was a relief to Rosie. Her uncle appeared prone to lapse into strange silences, as if he got lost in some mist, became disorientated and couldn't find his way out. It seemed to happen when he tried to recall the past.

There was one thing though that King Edmar did make clear to his niece: while she was with him, this castle was her home. It wasn't quite obvious to Rosie at first what this involved but it became clearer during her first encounter with the library.

At home there had been two libraries: one cluttered with papers and documents, with maps pinned to the wall, books in teetering piles all over every available surface, which her father had occupied as his study-library, and one with beautifully bound and elegant books on sumptuous shelves, offset with gold leaf, and charming tables occupied by elaborate floral displays, set next to suites of armchairs and sofas. Its floor was laid out with the most luxurious carpets. This latter library was stunning and breath-taking in its beauty but mostly shut, unless her mother was inclined to entertain literary visitors she meant to impress. Rosie had never been allowed in it on her own. Even when accompanied, she'd been strictly forbidden to touch anything. It wasn't that she had been allowed to touch things in her father's study-library but his door had always been open for her, provided she left things as she found them, and didn't disturb him when he was working.

The large library at her uncle's castle uncomfortably resembled that of her mother, with the difference that a great number of books, most of them as beautifully bound, looked as if they had actually left their shelves and been read. In addition to that, there was an upper gallery to her uncle's library, which was reached by spiral staircases, set on either end of the wide expanse of the room, and stretched all along the length of it. The large windows overlooked the drive. There were smaller free-standing bookshelves in between the huge wall of books and the sofas and armchairs that showed definite use. Each of the windows contained a window seat for reading. Rosie itched to go in and finally, after checking the coast was clear, she did.

Her exploration began tentatively, with an ear to the door in case the invitation, to make herself at home, hadn't included the library. She found a section on plants and natural history, great dusty-looking tomes by people whose names were repeated on several books in a row, books on art and history and so many other subjects. It was when she was trying to decide if there was something on the smaller shelves that she might like to read that she heard noises behind her. A short time later, a door opened in the middle of the wall of books and her uncle stepped out of what appeared to be a store cupboard.

It was her uncle who recovered first. Balancing some papers in one arm while pulling the door shut behind him, he ventured, "Found anything interesting?"

Rosie only nodded mutely, too stunned to say anything and wondering if she really ought to be here. Slightly awkward, but seemingly not at all put out by finding her there; her uncle came over to have a look.

"Herbaceous plants?" he asked.

"Yes," came a small voice, bracing for the onslaught.

"There are loads of those in the kitchen gardens if you'd like to have a look. We could go down there now?"

This was said in such a kind and gentle way that Rosie could only nod and smile weakly.

"You can leave that book out to check it later. It might be best if it stayed in the house though," her uncle said, more cheerfully now. He deposited his papers on one of the tables and beckoned to her. Striding down the corridor he kept talking about the plants they had, about someone called Cal, who grew and delivered a lot of them, and a lady of the most extraordinary talent for baking, whose rosemary bread they should sample one of these days.

He had not exaggerated. The kitchen gardens were crammed tight with plants. Coming out onto the terrace, her uncle had led her through the arched doorway to the left, absentmindedly patting one of the stone guardians on the head. The kitchen gardens were walled and every bed was neatly arranged with its plants labelled. Her uncle made her rub a leaf of lavender and inhale its scent and then they moved through, sampling some herbs by smell and taste. By the end of it Rosie felt so exhilarated that King Edmar had the impression of quite a different being occupying the slight frame.

"Choose some flowers for your room and I'll find a vase and take them up for you," he suggested and she did. "Now, if you'll excuse me, I must return to my papers," and with that he left her to explore by herself.

Once he had gone, Rosie collapsed on a bench under the shade of some trained fruit trees. It had been marvellous. With her father's main interest being botany, she had grown up with plants and flowers but had never been encouraged to have any in her room. It felt amazing. She wondered briefly if her uncle would keep his word but decided not to worry about it just now. Their talk on the way down had been the most relaxed she had had with him so far. Not only had he not minded finding her in the library, he had been pleased with it and enquired about her interests. He had also mentioned a cupboard full of jigsaws set under the highest of the window seats and told her to feel free to use any of the large library tables or the floor to spread them out. Sitting in the warmth of a sunny day, a contented sort of exhaustion set in and Rosie dozed off.

Birdsong and a quiet tapping noise, a bit further off, woke her. The dappled light made it easy for her eyes to adjust. Again she heard the tapping and suddenly a strange feeling overcame her. It was hard to describe, but it felt as if something deep inside was calling her, drawing her and she felt compelled to get up. She followed the path to the back of the garden and a small plain wooden door. Without thinking she turned the handle and pushed. No one appeared to have come this way for a long time. Weeds had grown up against the door and she had to shove quite hard before she was able to step through. Behind the door were the remnants of another garden. This one was surrounded by a low rounded wall against which holly and yew were growing from the other side. It felt hushed and sombre.

Unsure exactly why, Rosie set off towards the end of it and knelt down by a huge oak tree. A carpet of blue campanulas covered the floor by its roots and in between the growth the shape of a creature was just about visible. It was curled up, as if asleep, and a little smaller than a fully-grown cat. It seemed to have been made of bronze. Its large eyes were closed and the scales on its body were wrought in such elaborate detail that you could almost believe it could get up, yawn and breathe. From what Rosie could tell, she was looking at the sculpture of a pond dragon, a creature that had occasionally featured in some of her father's bedtime stories. It looked as if some artist had shared the same trove of stories.

Unable to resist, Rosie stretched out her finger and stroked the little dragon's head. A second later she leapt back with a yelp. For a moment, she had had the sensation of a powerful electric current coursing through her entire body.

But it wasn't that which made her run out of this part of the garden as quickly as she could. It was the fact that, when she had touched the statue, she hadn't felt bronze. It had felt as if she was touching a living, breathing creature, who – at any time now – would wake up to stretch languidly.

Running off, Rosie didn't see the small creature open its huge eyes and shake itself. This is a pity as pond dragons are very affectionate and curious – if slightly unruly – by nature and quite enjoy someone making a fuss over them. She also couldn't know that in the moment she had felt that electric current, a tousled-haired boy, sitting on a bench in the sunken garden with his arms folded across his chest and crossed legs stretched out into the path in front of him, woke up with a start.

4

THE HIDDEN SATCHEL

Supper and later bath time were somewhat subdued affairs that evening. During the meal her uncle had tried his best to engage her but – try as she might – Rosie was completely unable contribute anything. In the end he left her to her own thoughts and, wrapped up in them, they spent a quiet but not uncomfortable time. There didn't seem to be a need for explanations with her uncle. Rosie simply felt at ease with him. This was a new sensation for her.

What confused her though, was the way her whole body remembered the touch of that dragon. Instead of feeling unnerved, she now felt rather foolish for having fled the garden so abruptly. She wished she had taken a closer look at the creature with its slender body and short legs. Well, she could always go back and have a proper look tomorrow.

It was when she came up from her bath that she remembered those flowers she had picked in the kitchen gardens earlier. Entering her room, Rosie discovered a small round glass vase, standing on a pretty little doily on her desk. It was made from exquisite white cloth and covered with tiny pink bush roses and bluebells. Next to it a book from the library lay with a short note saying "Dear Rosie, I've marked the pages with your flowers in case you want to read up on them". Underneath was a small symbol. Rosie was extremely pleased with this. Hugging Sir Redhill to her, she climbed into bed and almost immediately fell into a deep sleep.

It was later that night, way past midnight, that she woke up. Snippets of dreams were still clinging to edge of her mind, with images of flowers and gardens slowly receding. She wasn't sure what had woken her or if she even was properly awake but she suddenly had the distinctive feeling that she wasn't alone. She could definitely sense another presence in the room. Clutching Sir Redhill tightly and without making even the slightest sound she peeped out from among her covers. What she saw nearly made her gasp out loud.

There, in the corner of her room and bathed in bright moonlight falling through the window, a boy was kneeling on the floor. He had his back to her and was exactly in her line of vision from the bed. He seemed to be working swiftly across the panelling. A brief spell later there was a click and then a panel slid aside, leaving a hidden cavity exposed to view. Carefully the boy took something from his shoulder and pushed it inside before sliding the panel back in its place. That done, he got up, crossed the room swiftly and left by the door, which closed noiselessly behind him. Rosie lay there, mind racing. Before she could puzzle things out though, she fell – still confused – back into sleep. It was very late the next morning when she finally woke up again.

You can't think on an empty stomach and the night's events had taken it out of Rosie. She had a large bowl of porridge with fruit and two scrambled eggs, washed down with a mug of tea. After that she felt ready to go up and tackle her room. It had certainly been bizarre but there was probably a very logical explanation for what had happened last night. Given that Mrs Baird had said on their trip into town that there were no other children besides her at the castle, Rosie felt sure that it had just been a weird dream. She had after all been overwhelmed by everything that had happened to her recently and her mother had always deplored her fanciful imagination. Still, Rosie was determined to see if there was perhaps a secret panel after all. It could come in handy.

The panelling looked solid. Pushing here and there yielded absolutely no result. She tapped the surface and although it did sound a little hollow, it did that in various places and not just where she had seen the boy kneel. About to give up, something caught her eye. Most of the panelling was plain but – just above the skirting rail – running along the bottom was a small line of carvings. It made no sense for them to be that low, as you could hardly see them, but there they were. She leaned in for a closer inspection. The decorations in the corner of one panel were definitely slightly different from the rest. There, in among the masses of intricately carved roses, leaves, grapes and butterflies, nestled a tiny dragon. It reminded her of the one on the handle of the spoon she had used the evening of her arrival. A small shiver ran through her. Like the dragon on the spoon that first night, this one appeared to wink at her. It was there for a split second and then it was gone. On impulse she reached out and touched the dragon, which slid inwards and disappeared with a soft click. At the same moment the panel slid smoothly aside, revealing the same cavity she had glimpsed in the middle of the night. Hidden inside it was a worn brown leather satchel.

Old habits die hard. So the first thing she did following her discovery was to latch the door to her room to ensure that no one could come in uninvited. Then she picked up the satchel and sat, legs crossed, on her bedspread. Unbuckling the clasp Rosie had a brief sensation of movement, almost as if the satchel had shifted slightly under her hands. Cautiously she opened the flap and peered inside. The entire interior appeared to be taken up with a large rectangular object wrapped in embroidered cloth. Tucked inside it was a piece of old parchment.

Holding it out in front of her Rosie could make out the faint words 'To the heir' at the top of the paper. Underneath were strange scratches that resembled the traces of birds' feet, as if a small army of them had marched across the paper. Slightly mystified, she put it aside and carefully unwound the cloth from the object beneath until she was holding a book. Now this was interesting. Why was it hidden away here and not kept in her uncle's library?

A pattern of rainbow colours playing across its cover brought her attention back to it. It must have been a trick of the light because the cover, though not plain, was a definite shade of golden red. Rosie exhaled slowly. With a slight tingling in the palms of her hands, she carefully opened it. The flyleaf was a greenish bronze with a pattern of droplets running into one another. It was mesmerising. Shaking herself out of her trance, she quickly turned to the title page which stated in clear letters 'Mari's Book of Dragons and their Magic.'

Rosie frowned. Dragons? Magic? Did this person really believe in dragons and that they had magic? Any fairy tale would tell you that they could spit fire, fly and carried the dragon shingles but magic? A huge wave of disappointment rose up inside her, threatening to engulf her in misery. After all the excitement of last night's dream, then actually finding part of it to be true, she was landed with nothing but a ridiculous collection of make believe. Someone, maybe this Mari, might find that entertaining but she, Rosie, felt completely let down.

As she made to close the book, she caught a glimmer of colour out of the corner of her eye. There, leaning against the curtain by the window, was the boy with tousled brown hair. He looked strangely insubstantial and upset. A shiver of recognition ran through her. This was the same boy she had seen last night. In that moment he caught her eye and briefly held her gaze. A second later she blinked and he was gone.

There was a rushing in her ears and her heart was pounding. She gripped the book tightly and tried to take some calming breaths, counting to ten as taught by her father. It was when she had reached seven that she heard whispering and laughter coming from the book. No longer caring that she couldn't understand this and no longer in any state to mind, she turned over the front page decisively and found herself face to face with a dragon.

Instead of getting another shock, a smile spread across her face. The dragon's green eyes were crinkled good-naturedly and his face looked as if he was laughing. A warm glow came from him. Distracted by this it took a while before Rosie noticed a small caption underneath the picture 'Uncle Alfred after winning the annual garden show'. She blinked. A garden show? While her bewildered brain was still trying to make sense of what she had seen and read, Rosie's hands took charge and closed the book. She got off the bed and stowed the book, parchment and satchel back in the cavity behind the panel. Whoever this Mari was, and she felt almost certain that it was a boy, he had obviously had a very vivid imagination and decided to make up a book about dragons. The picture had been done by someone with a great talent to paint though. It had felt so real. Leaving the room and the puzzle of the book behind her, Rosie set off towards the gardens, to hopefully clear her mind.

5

Nymphette

THE WORRIES OF KING EDMAR

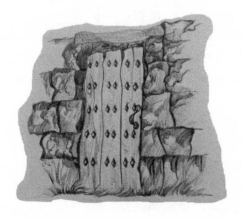

From an upper window King Edmar saw his niece take off into the grounds. It was peculiar to see her tear off like that. She had changed a lot in the weeks since she'd arrived or maybe not changed as much as come out of her shell. He had never been fond of his sister and his niece's behaviour when she had first arrived, neglected and almost flinching, had reinforced that dislike again. He wondered how his brother-in-law had fared. His Aunt Eleanor had had her thoughts on the marriage but King Edmar himself had been far too poorly to feel greatly interested in anything at the time things were arranged.

That was then and now things were beginning to catch up with him. The signs were giving him a year at the most before his time was up. A year to solve the conundrum or go down with it and there was no one to guide him; no one who knew the intricacies of the problem. Even worse there were no records or memories. Every time he tried to go back to the time before matters spun out of control he was met by a wall of mist. It was as if his mind was guarding something it refused to give up. If only he could remember but he knew it was futile to try. The castle had never willingly given up secrets it liked to keep and it looked as if part of his past was locked to him.

In the end what would happen would happen and all he could do was try to put safeguards in place to see his niece would be fine afterwards. He had a year he told himself. With that in mind, he locked the door to his chambers and went over to kneel by one of the trunks at the left-hand wall. Carefully he lifted out the materials that he knew would help him settle. With his hands working methodically, he gradually relaxed, even cheering up slightly.

Rosie meanwhile had reached the end of the lawn and crossed the grassy meadow that lay beyond it. She was leaning against a rowan tree in order to steady herself, while catching her breath, and felt extremely vexed. Why hadn't the boy stopped? She had seen him running through the park and shouted after him. He had even turned around briefly before simply carrying on, and now he was gone. Where on earth was he?

She scanned the view in front of her, noticing the way the land fell away as if from a small edge, but couldn't see him anywhere. It was as if he had vanished into thin air. It was aggravating too, he either wanted to be friends or he didn't. Rosie really wished he'd make up his mind. She looked around again. There was nothing about to give her a clue. The lawn behind her was empty and the grass of the meadow wasn't high enough to hide anyone, even if they were lying down. Diagonally to her left was the wood belonging to the palace grounds and to her right, a bit further off, was another clump of trees. But there was no sign of anyone apart from herself.

Again she had that peculiar feeling of something not being quite right settling on her. She turned her head first towards the castle woods, forbidding in their gloom, and then to the little wood on her right. Was it just her imagination or did the wood on the right seem so much more cheerful and brighter than the one to her left? Trying to gather her thoughts she looked down and noticed that there was a strange pattern, like boundary markings, running right along where she was standing. She bent down and touched it. It felt bit like a very low wall or a slightly raised path and appeared to be quite old. She wondered if it led anywhere. The easiest way was probably to follow the path in one direction and find out.

It took longer than she had thought to reach the castle's woods. She had decided on that way first as, though less inviting, it was closer and she could always go and explore the other wood at some later point. There was something about the castle wood that drew her. In addition to that, the strange path she had discovered led unerringly towards it.

When she reached the first trees the path changed. From here on it was covered in part by grey-green moss, the glaze of the coloured bricks barely visible. After a brief hesitation she set off into the wood. Despite the thickening undergrowth, the path itself was easy to follow. It led straight through some shady part of the wood, where things seemed to be moving along between the trees. Rosie didn't dare stay still long enough to make out what exactly they were.

At some point she heard some mournful cry but that seemed to be further away and may just have been the call of some bird. She carried on until she came to a clearing. At the other end, opposite from where she had come, was a red door set into a stone wall. So there was something in this wood and where there was a door there was usually something that lay behind it. Excited, she rushed towards it and tried the handle. It was locked. It would have been too good if it had just opened.

She stepped back and focussed her attention on the door. It was made from thick planks of woods and had been painted red, though the paint was peeling away in some places. Moving closer again she noticed a small sign with worn writing stating that this was 'Leonora's Gate'. She tried to look through the crack above the door but couldn't see anything. She tried the handle again, first right and then left just in case it opened the opposite way from the usual doors, but it stayed shut. This was frustrating. What was the point in discovering a door to something that looked suspiciously like a garden and if you couldn't get through it?

She considered her options. The wall didn't look that high and, walking along it some way, there were cracks in between the stones, just big enough for a smaller foot to fit. Slowly she started to climb. A moment later, triumphantly, she pulled herself up onto the top of the wall. She steadied herself, peered down and started to scream.

6

Nymphette

THE SEA CAVE

Less than five minutes later Rosie collapsed on a bench in the shrubbery. She had absolutely no idea how she had managed to get down that wall so quickly and without hurting herself. She had run helter-skelter out of the wood without stopping, intent only to put as much distance as possible between herself and that thing. It was only when she broke out into the sunlight that she turned round to see if anything was following her. To her great relief there wasn't. So she had run back up the meadow and lawn as fast as her legs would carry her. At last she put her head between her legs to get her breath back. Then, without warning, she burst into tears.

It took Rosie a while to get a grip on herself but, after a good deal of crying and thorough use of the handkerchief Mrs Baird had insisted she carry in her pockets, she succeeded. This was ridiculous! Was she to spend her entire time at this place panicking and running away? For the first time in her life she had a chance to genuinely explore somewhere real and all she had done so far was being worried and scared and unsure. Her father had always told her to trust herself more. He had also told her that they descended from an absolutely fearless ancestor. Rosie would be a complete fool if she let this castle's tricks defeat her!

Shaking her head determinately she sat up and checked her pockets to put away the crumpled handkerchief. Her hand brushed against something coarse. Attached to the material of her cardigan were three seedpods of the variety that relies on carriers to spread it, lodging themselves in animal furs or, in this case, clinging to the material of her clothes. She pulled them off carefully and examined them.

Their colour was strange. The outer part, the one that attached itself, consisted of some hairy reddish fibres. Checking them more closely she realised that each contained a small roundish seed. After gently rolling them between her fingers she finally had three small tear drops in her palm. They were golden, streaked with a rich bronze and a dark green. Rosie had never come across seeds like these before. Not even her father's extensive collections had held anything similar. Excitement bubbled through her. What if they were something as yet undiscovered?

After a moment of this elation though, she deflated. What if her uncle or Mrs Baird just threw them away like her mother had done so often with things she had brought back inside to keep? She absolutely didn't want these beautiful seeds to end up in the rubbish. Staring into space, lost in thought, it suddenly hit her. There were gardens here, weren't there? Close to those kitchen gardens was a potting shed. She had briefly glanced into it on her tour of the house and grounds. There might be something in there that wouldn't be missed. All she needed was a pot and some soil. Carefully stowing the seeds in the empty pocket of her cardigan she set off.

It was later that evening, long after supper. Rosie was sitting at her desk – with a deep red plant pot on a coaster in front of her – leafing through yet another library book. With her uncle's permission to help herself to what she wanted from the library, she had returned to her room with an armful of books. So far nothing had turned up. This was perhaps understandable, as all she had was a description of the seeds and she might easily have overlooked something.

But she had been right about the kitchen gardens' potting shed. After a short search, she had found some extremely dusty but colourful pots of red, burnt orange and yellow on one of the shelves at the back. Deciding on the red pot to bring on the seeds and the other ones in case they germinated and needed more space, she had planted her three seeds in a neat little triangle in the red pot and taken the other ones to her room for later. They were stored on the bottom shelf of the near empty bookcase. The potting shed had had several bays full of pots and tables to work on and getting her hands on earth had not been difficult. Now all she had to do was to wait for the seeds to sprout.

Sighing, Rosie finally put down the last book – nothing. It wasn't that she had seriously expected to find a record but, deep down, she had still hoped. Turning her head sideways while stretching, her gaze fell on the panelling. Perhaps she should have another look at Mari's book just in case it mentioned anything useful.

Half an hour later she had made no inroads on the book but that didn't matter. Poring over a map spread out in front of her, Rosie was making more discoveries in a short space of time than she had during her entire tour of the castle grounds and library. The map, which had been stored, neatly folded, inside the book's first few pages not only gave an overview of the castle grounds but also the immediate surroundings up to the coast. Marked on it were roads, lanes and paths showing access to coves and beaches, along with other points of interest and accompanied by a clear legend to help her understand the various symbols. A number of places in particular aroused her interest. Folding the map and storing it in a compartment in the satchel that seemed made for it, she stowed the book, wrapped in its cloth, back in its previous hiding place. Tomorrow, she decided as she pulled up her covers and turned over to sleep, she would explore the coast.

Resting the map on the handlebars of her bike, Rosie tried to orientate herself again. So far everything had been fairly easy to follow. She studied the stretch ahead against the map and found the fork marked on it seemed to match the slightly overgrown lane on her left. Stowing the map away safely, she set off.

From out of the high grass to the side of the road a large pair of grass-green eyes followed her progress. Then the small creature on four short legs went after her.

She left her bike in the long grass at the top of the headland. In front of her a sandy path snaked down. It led to an outcrop of black octagonal rocks. Climbing down carefully, she came to a very narrow but clear-cut path running the length of that particular headland. Into the rock, at the parts close to sea, handholds, threaded through with a rope, had been fitted long ago. She walked straight down and felt the path rise slightly before stopping at an outcrop of rocks, petering out into the sea in front of her. To her left the path curved inward. After taking a couple of deep steadying breaths, she went inside.

The sea cave was spacious, in some ways bigger than Rosie had expected, but in in other ways a lot smaller too. She couldn't quite express it. The ceiling, sparkling at the entrance with light reflected from the water and the paler stone, was darkened in some places, while clear and uncovered in others. She squinted back at the path she had come from. It suddenly looked a long way back.

The sound of the water within the cave was fascinating, soothing – due to the rhythm of the rolling sea – but slightly haunting too. It was as if this cave was not only a place but almost an entrance or portal to another world. In a certain way it felt as if, without making any actual sound, the walls were whispering to her. Something they and she knew was important but, at the same time, one party couldn't quite articulate and the other party couldn't quite make out yet.

She put her hand to the inside wall of the cave, feeling its cool smooth stone beneath her fingers. There was a story here; she could feel that something important had gone on here, something forgotten in the mist of time but still influencing the present. There was some sort of connection; a meaning to her life but it was too obscure to be made out. It was confusing, fascinating and extremely vexing at the same time. She looked towards the mouth of the cave and out to the sky. Birds were circling in the distance. How would it feel to see a dragon wheel across that sky, she wondered. For a brief moment, she almost saw it, a great blue dragon whirling gracefully through the air, dark against the powdery blue. She clung to that image and suddenly an eye, with a slit pupil, flashed past her inner vision. She blinked. It had been so clear it startled her. Once there were dragons...

She shook her head. Dragons. Even here by the sea there seemed to be no escape from the castle's madness. If that was the case why wasn't she some princess in one of her father's fairy tales instead of this girl in boyish clothes, heartily disapproved of and possibly disliked by her mother, who had cycled half the morning to end up in a cave by the sea? Even more a sea cave that seemed to know things and whisper them half-understood into her ears? What had made her pick it out on the map and follow this path?

Lost in her musings, her eyes caught at the clear water at the bottom of the cave, so clear the rocks below, pale and smooth, were visible. The perfect water to swim in, if it wasn't for the fact that it kept surging back and forth in a sucking motion that would ensure anything in it would get battered against the rocks. That thought, however fleeting, made her shiver and then, realising that she must have been out here for quite a considerable amount of time and was beginning to feel cold, she left.

It was probably good that she was already quite far away by the time the sigh came. Had she heard it she might have panicked. It is also reasonable to assume that it would have ruined any prospects of future visits to the cave. So it was probably also most helpful, that Rosie didn't know that opposite where she had stood and touched the stone an eye now opened in the rock and blinked once. It was probably best too that she didn't know that the eye, bronze-green with a slit pupil, was following her steady progress back up the hillside to retrieve her bike. It was an eye that sat in the head of an unseen creature, who found all this very interesting indeed.

7

Nymphette

FOOTPRINTS IN THE SAND

The map had indicated not only the sea cave but also a beach and a ruin. As places, all three of these were familiar to Rosie from stories her father had told her when she was little. It was on a path, coming up from the exploration of a sea cave, that he had met her mother and known that she was the one he was destined to marry. Pressed for a reason he had always said simply that he knew.

In the last years, that story had hardly ever been told. What Rosie heard instead, behind closed doors, were raised voices, then shouting, then the smashing of china, followed by the uncontrollable howling – and not even remotely ladylike – rage of her mother. Things had got worse in the months before her father disappeared and her mother entered her own world. Rosie had sought refuge in her father's library, playing almost noiselessly behind the high sofa where she felt safe.

There were scuff marks on the map close to the ruin but Rosie was more interested in the beach anyway. Wheeling her bike along the rough path, she reached the dune above the beach. To her left, towards the sea cave, water was spouting up in a plume of spray from between dark rocks. Stretched out at her feet, lay a long stretch of white beach. To her right, sitting on a tidal island in the sea, was a squat tower and further back traces of the ruin. With the tide in, the island was currently completely cut off from the mainland. Maybe it was her imagination but it had a slightly sinister feel to it.

A flicker of movement down below caught her eye and she was only just in time to see a sleek creature streak off the beach and dash into the coarse grass in the dunes. It had roughly the shape of an otter but there was something odd about it, the colour for once. Hoping that it had left some tracks Rosie sidled down the sandy path towards the beach.

There were footprints there but she wasn't positive they were those of an otter. They were roughly the right size but didn't appear to be as webbed and the claws seemed daintier somehow.

The distance between them indicated a slightly smaller creature too. It was puzzling. Retracing its steps brought her closer to the shore. In the middle of one of those wet imprints she noticed something gleam. Rubbing lightly with her finger at the sand she felt something hard and smooth. A pebble maybe. She brushed aside more of the sand and a shape emerged. Inserting her fingernail under the edge, it caught, ever so slightly, lifting the object. Wriggling a bit more, a small plopping noise announced that the object had come out. She lifted it triumphantly and stared. It appeared to be a piece of jewellery, shaped like a tear drop, tarnished with age.

She turned it over to examine it more closely and nearly dropped it in surprise. The tip was formed of a dragon's head which was met at the back by the end of its own tail while its body, hanging below it, formed the shape of a boat with tiny shields. The dragon's top and bottom front teeth were visible in its snout and it seemed to be smiling but that wasn't what had shaken Rosie. It was more that this dragon, like the one on the cutlery on her first night and the other one in the panelling, seemed to have winked at her in a friendly and conspiratorial kind of fashion.

She stared at it hard but the movement had gone. Maybe it had just been a trick of the light reflected from the water. Whatever had happened though, she desperately wanted to keep this dragon boat pendant. It felt like a friendly weight in her hand and she felt the urge to carry it with her, as if for protection. There was no one around but her and some seabirds. No one to ask but there was absolutely no way that she was going to drop this little dragon back onto the sand and leave it behind. Stowing it safely in the inner pocket of her satchel, she turned round and left the beach. A pair of grass-green eyes followed her. Then, task done, their owner yawned luxuriously, curled up in a little circle and fell asleep.

By the time Rosie, exhausted from her trip, was back at the castle and helping herself to food from the pantry shelf Mrs Baird kept stocked for luncheons, a red-haired woman was making her way down to the white beach. Her name was Lucinda Adgryphorus and she was soon to take possession of Sea View House. A distant relative had left it to her in their will.

Having recently completed the final showcasing of her apprentice-ship, gaining her the coveted Master of the Arts title, with the highest distinction, she was looking forward to working quietly on her own for a while.

The old house stood on a green rise above the sea, visible inland from the distance. It had been built with its front facing the sea, looking out across it with the spouting cave to the left and the tidal island with remnants of an old castle to the right. On clear days you could see the islands – even the faraway Dragon's Point – in the distance.

It had been almost twenty years since Lucinda had last been out here. When she was younger, she had stayed four consecutive summers with her grandmother in town, occasionally sallying forth into the royal gardens with the town's gardener Cal. Those had been happy times. Now she was on the cusp of a new life. Working in this part of the country would enable her to take stock first, instead of plunging headlong into a busy new life. Despite a number of stipulations made in her relative's will, such as living in the house for at least a year and 'observe the coast' – whatever that meant – the monetary provision that came with it was extremely generous. Lucinda wasn't lavish in her spending but certain artists' materials were costly. She fully intended to use her breathing space wisely and hopefully gain some patronage in town. All those details were hazy still. For the time being the house was finally ready for habitation, the workmen had packed up and she was on her way down to the beach for a quiet moment, before returning to her grandmother's for one last fortnight before the move.

She noticed the tracks almost immediately and briefly considered but dismissed them as otters'. Curious though they were her interest was more on the other tracks, which were those of a child. Despite the lure of the ruins and the sea cave close by, local children rarely came here. They usually got as far as the rise before becoming inexplicably terrified and turning round. From the look of it the child had followed the creature's tracks down to the shore before leaving the beach. It seemed as if, maybe, the observation part of the task alluded to by her relative had already begun.

8

THE TRESPASSER

Rosie wasn't tempted to return to the coast any time soon after her first visit. The ride down being exhausting certainly played some part in it, but there was also a niggling worry about the pendant. What if someone was still looking for it? She hadn't stolen it, but someone might want it back. Again and again she examined it, all polished now, and then told herself – also over and over – that it had obviously been lying there for such a long time that it was highly unlikely the owner would come back to claim it. Apart from that, it felt so right, resting

36

against her skin below her collarbone, a friendly weight just like she had imagined it to be. In a box of trinkets her uncle had given her to look through one rainy day, saying "If anything takes your fancy, keep it," she had found a thin but strong short silver chain, which had proven the perfect match for her little dragon boat. She took care to ensure it was covered by clothes as much as possible. Despite the fact that she didn't really think it would happen with her uncle, she vividly remembered her mother's sharp reprimands not to wear jewellery on non-occasions-days, something she herself had been exempt from.

A fortnight after her terrifying encounter on the locked garden's wall, and after checking the coast was clear, she risked another trip to the potting shed and separated out her three tiny seedlings into individual pots. It was impossible to tell yet what they were going to be but their roots looked extremely promising and they were forming neat clusters of crooked leaves. Rosie was rather proud of her achievement. She was cautious though and kept her plants and her dragon pendant to herself.

The one thing that put a slight dampener on her new-found happiness was a discovery in the overgrown part of the grounds, adjacent to the kitchen gardens. After daring herself to go back to touch it again she found, to her dismay, that the statue of the pond dragon was gone. Apart from that the castle and its upper gardens were becoming more and more like home.

When asked, her uncle had said, vaguely, that he had seen some papers around but he hadn't elaborated. Rosie felt it was high time for her to finally find out some more about the history of the castle. She was therefore – once again – planning to scour the library.

Meanwhile, in the lower parts of the gardens, far from prying eyes, a stranger had taken up residence. No one really saw him arrive. One morning there was just an old overgrown vegetable patch in a dilapidated garden, which used to hold a tiny seasonal cottage; the next morning smoke could be seen, rising from the old chimney, curling gently down towards the sea. Over the course of the next weeks, anyone curious enough to observe the goings on would have seen the greenhouses slowly regain their former appearance, though some of the broken glass was replaced with rather odd colourful little panes. A compost heap grew under the old oak tree opposite which neat rows of vegetable beds took shape. The casual observer might also have noticed that the orchard in the northwest corner of the garden was slowly emerging again with undergrowth being removed and the old trees, relieved of some of their dead wood, starting to resemble their dapper old selves again.

The new occupant had arrived in the middle of summer – an odd time – and he wasn't exactly sure why he had come to this place. He could sense a sadness that was only just being contained lurk behind the old border. Something told him that this was the place for him to be but he wasn't entirely sure about the timing or the shape or form his future would take. For now he simply concentrated on gardening and, particularly compared to the soil he was used to, this was as good as any place, perhaps even better, to start in. More importantly, for the first time in his life, he felt as if he properly belonged somewhere.

9

Nymphette

THE ONCE MOST
ELIGIBLE BACHELOR

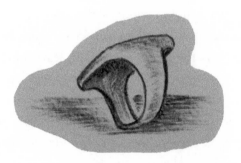

It was mid-week. King Edmar was engaged on business, Rosie was –
unsuccessfully – searching the library, the stranger was gardening and,
in town, Lucinda was carrying a small wooden trunk through the archway of a cobbled courtyard. A basket of bakery goods and crate of
grocery supplies had already been stowed away carefully. She pushed
the trunk under the bench at the front and climbed up to sit next to
Cal. She waved cheerfully at her grandmother, standing at the door to
the café, and then the cart was moving.

Today she was moving into Sea View House. Cal had errands at
the castle and – as even with a wagon attached, it would be extremely
laborious for Lucinda to get the last things over by bike – she had gratefully accepted the offer of a lift. She knew Cal was curious to see the

old house too and it had been a long time since they had had a chance to catch up. So the round trip was not unwelcome to either of them.

There was one piece of information in particular Lucinda was hoping to glean from him. While in town and preparing for her move, she had become aware of rumours about the king. She knew from her grandmother that he had been on the throne for more than a decade and that – generally – people respected him greatly. Most subjects were content with the way he looked after the country's affairs. It wasn't governance that people – if they did at all – complained about, it was more the lack of the king's presence, a queen and perhaps even more particularly an heir. There were children, who could not really remember ever having clasped eyes on the king, so rarely did he attend great public engagements. Rumour had it he was cursed.

The day was bright and the skies clear. You could already see that the sun would burn away the morning's haze to leave a beautiful summer's day in its wake. Lucinda enjoyed the light breeze coming in from the sea. That evening she planned to sit on the bench, overlooking the white beach by Sea View House, and watch the waves come in.

Her mind turned back to the king. Wondering how to broach the subject she glanced at Cal and found him giving her a shrewd appraising look.

"I suspect you've heard the rumours, lass," he said cheerfully, "about our King Edmar and the curse."

"Was it really that obvious?"

Cal chuckled and said "The question was burnt on your forehead from the moment your grandmother sighed after mentioning his name."

Feeling she might as well come out with it straightaway she demanded, "What happened? All I've picked up is that the king was once considered the most eligible bachelor and now people, well especially the mothers of marriageable daughters, act as if their daughters had a lucky escape. His country is prosperous, the majority of roads are well maintained, trade is flourishing, peace contracts are signed and he has been on the throne for more than a decade. My grandmother also says that he has none of the airs and graces his parents and sister had, so what is going on? Some people talk of him in hushed voices as if he's afflicted or on his deathbed or both."

Cal considered her. He had always been fond of Amelia's granddaughter, seeing her sitting in her grandmother's café or garden, almost always drawing. She might come from 'out of town' but her connection with the land ran deep. It was palpable. He had not been at all surprised to find out that it was her who had been named as heir to Sea View House. It fitted. There was a strong undercurrent running its course whose aim wasn't clear yet. He only hoped it was good.

Feeling her gaze on him still – the question hanging in the air – he kept his eyes on the road and told her the story as it had been circulated around town.

It wasn't quite true that no one had seen the king in the last years. He had a circle of advisors and stewards who had regular communications with him and occasionally acted on his behalf. While it was true that his country, as she had remarked, was peaceful and prosperous the king himself had not really attended many public functions since a year after his ascent to the throne more than a decade ago. People still occasionally talked about their king's lavish coronation and how incredibly handsome the young king had looked. Women especially got a faraway look in their eyes when remembering the stunning contrast his thick, wavy, chestnut brown dark hair had made on the dark red royal robes. Some, when remembering the day, would start to describe his eyes with an excited giggle in their voices but funnily everyone seemed to agree that, though splendid, the king had not looked particularly happy. He hadn't exactly scowled or looked cold but he hadn't smiled a lot either during the entire ceremony. Some folk recalled that he had actually appeared extremely upset when presented with the royal insignia, as if burdened beyond measure. The realm's signet ring, an ancient heirloom to the kingdom – a most precious object, inlaid with a delicate pattern of a curled up dragon forming a perfect circle – had almost brought tears to his eyes. The dragon, glowing in varying hues of burning orange, red, gold, green and blue depending on the light that fell on it, was covered by a clear and allegedly indestructible substance which allowed its wearer to use the ring as a seal without incurring any damage to the image itself. It was regarded an absolute masterpiece of craftsmanship and symbolised continuance and prosperity of the kingdom. The king had taken his oath to protect the land and to uphold its laws in a grave voice and the celebrations had concluded with the ceremonial banquet.

Everything seemed set on course but then, about a year after the coronation and the king attending numerous of the illustrious gatherings his position demanded of him, things had begun to go awry.

King Edmar, as would happen to any handsome young bachelor with a kingdom but without an intended, had been repeatedly invited by the highest and most noble lords of his realm. In addition to that, princes and kings from countries over the seas invited him into their houses but strangely, at some point, the king had begun to turn down every single invitation.

Undaunted by this, there continued to be a stream of veritable tours to the castle with countless young women parading most becomingly up and down by the castle gates but to no avail; none of them were ever asked to come into the king's presence.

After a while, people, the Bellescombes in particular – distant cousins of the late queen – had grown rather impatient. What was the point of having a handsome and more importantly *single* monarch when he so obviously considered himself too good for any of their daughters? A certain stratum within society, namely one consisting of parents with unmarried daughters and those daughters themselves, were starting to get extremely disgruntled with the king's behaviour when suddenly the most dismaying news from the castle reached the towns and villages of the kingdom.

Rumour had it – and you could hear the shocked intake of breath when word spread on the marketplaces and in the taverns – that on some imprudent travel abroad a while after his coronation ('That's what you get from venturing into foreign climes!') their king had been cursed. This spread like wildfire, questions were asked and finally at the height of the speculations the castle's heralds appeared.

Some old witch, angry no doubt that the king had refused to marry her warty daughter when there were maidens of the most exquisite beauty in his own realm (so beautiful and exquisite indeed that our poor king had not known how to choose among them), had put a cruel curse on their beloved monarch. Within months of this meeting, our noble and most handsome king, the castle's heralds proclaimed, had aged and become withered. It was a most gruesome sight to behold that the king did not wish to inflict purposely on any of his noble subjects.

The proclamation went on to say that the witch had warned the king that his condition would spread to any woman who became his bride. With a heavy heart the king had therefore chosen to bear this sad state alone. The poor heralds were pressed for further information and numerous suggestions were made, with fortune tellers being employed, but nothing helped. It was only now that it was noted that a dark and unhappy gloom was hanging over the castle and all its grounds. It was remarked that it seemed to stop at the border of the royal premises and it was therefore deemed unsafe, yes unhealthy even, to venture towards the castle.

People would talk sagely of the curse and congratulate themselves on their own or their daughter's or niece's or ward's lucky escape. Some girl, who like so many others had secretly been assured that she would pocket the king eventually, was even so bold as to suggest defiantly that this whole affair was the king's own fault. Had he chosen a wife before running into the witch, none of this would have happened and he would still be able to show his handsome face. True, the men in the taverns and the women at their evening entertainments agreed, it was the king's own indecision that was to blame for his still being an eligible bachelor when he ran into that witch. Some girls, who had, funnily enough, wasted hours striding up and down in front of the castle gates tossing their hair, now said that they had never really been that interested in him in the first place. One even pointed out that marriage to a king like that, who so easily attracted a witch's displeasure, could have led to your child being cursed the first time you proudly presented it to the world and what a mess that would have been.

"So apart from business he has in town, the odd ceremony or appointment, he very much keeps himself to himself," Cal finished.

Lucinda, mulling this over, wondered what he wasn't telling her.

"He may look ancient but he's very competent," he muttered into the silence that had now sprung up between them.

There were some parts that didn't quite add up but he had ended such a solemn note that she didn't want to ask any more questions, especially as the castle itself was now coming into view.

What he hadn't told her was of his own unease. It was that he did not fully believe the story or at least not this version of it. He felt, deep down, there was something more sinister at work and had the very strong feeling that their king was slowly beginning to run out of time.

THE STRANGER IN THE GARDEN

Once they had passed through the castle gates into the grounds, they took the less formal path, which split off from the main entrance to the right-hand side. Through the line of trees on her left Lucinda caught a glimpse of the castle's front, the stonework golden in the early morning sun. Cal brought the cart to a halt at the lower end of the kitchen gardens, where they started to unload.

Lucinda wasn't familiar with the part this close to the castle. When she was younger she had occasionally set foot into the castle grounds but that had only ever been to the lower gardens and parkland. She was itching to go and have a look but knew that casual visitors were un-likely to be encouraged. The king obviously valued his privacy. At that moment Cal came over to her, carrying a small crate full of daisies.

"Could you perhaps take these down to the sunken garden?" he asked. "They seem unusually busy today."

Lucinda didn't mind at all. She was glad to have a chance to have a quick look around. Following Cal's instructions she found her way to the garden easily. It was when she was already on the steps leading down, wondering where she should leave the plants, that she realised there was someone in it. A man was sitting on a bench, crossed legs stretched out casually and arms folded behind his head, his face tipped up towards the sun. Her first impression was of someone with white hair, but coming closer it became obvious, that that had been down to a shimmer of the morning light.

He was about her age, clad in boots, a pair of dark trousers and a jumper from which a shirt collar peaked out. Despite the tip of his head, an unruly lock of dark hair had fallen into his forehead. For a busy castle this man was quite at his leisure. As if he had suddenly picked up on her presence, he dropped his arms and looked around, catching sight of her on the steps.

"Oh, good morning," he gave her a broad smile. "No one told me we had engaged a new under-gardener."

There was something about the appraising look he gave her, as well as the way he was quizzically raising an eyebrow while saying this, that unfortunately made Lucinda's blood boil. In the time of her apprentice-ship she had met enough of this type with their careless good looks, but lazy and forever making assumptions about her. She held on to her crate and said, "Cal asked me to bring these down. He said everyone seemed rather busy." she couldn't help adding a little pointedly.

To her great surprise, he was completely unfazed and instead burst out laughing.

"They always are," he brought out with tears of merriment in his eyes. "Fact is," he added, sobering up and coming over, "they are afraid of this garden. They think it's cursed," he added musingly, bending over the crate to inspect the plants.

Lucinda watched the almost yearning expression in his face while he studied the daisies, gently touching their petals, tracing them with the tip of his index finger. For a split second he looked so very vulnerable that she felt something like pity well up inside her.

Until he spoilt it all by leaning back and saying "Well, I suppose we'll see how long they live" in an offhand sort of way that really annoyed her. It took a lot of willpower not to shove the crate at him. It was only the thought that he might drop it, with the daisies coming off badly or that he might complain to the king, which might get Cal into trouble, that made her lower the crate – with extreme care – onto the nearest bench and leave. Still seething, she didn't bother to acknowledge his "goodbye" as she stalked off, back towards the cart.

The brisk walk burnt off most of her anger. By the time she reached Cal again, she was feeling a little less disgruntled.

"Met someone down that way?" Cal asked in an innocent voice which somehow told Lucinda that he knew the answer.

"Yes," she nodded grimly.

"He's not half as bad as he seems," said Cal cheerfully while they clambered onto the cart. "He tries very hard."

Lucinda didn't trust herself to speak.

"He's been in the sunken garden close to the lawn nearly every time I've delivered plants recently, looking simultaneously hopeful and upset."

Lucinda couldn't help let out a small noise that had a slight touch of derision in it.

Cal laughed at her scowl and – setting the cart in motion – said "If he got your back up I would try to let it go, lass. Doesn't get you any-where and keeps me in business." He chortled and they continued the next stage of their journey in silence.

Later that day, after Cal had left, Lucinda was sitting outside, overlooking the white beach and tried to piece it all together. The more she thought about it, the less it made sense to her. It was as if she was blocked by something to go further back. She did remember the gardens and her summers spent with her grandmother and even some trips out here to Sea View House but somehow she had the feeling that there was something or someone else that eluded her.

Cal's story of the cursed king had jarred in her mind. It wasn't that she didn't believe the reports about the King Edmar's most appallingly withered state but it was more that she didn't think that the castle's melancholy that Cal's story referred to was that recent. In fact, now that she thought of it, the grounds had felt different that last summer she had stayed with her grandmother. But there was something else, buried deeply in her memory. Well, she knew that whatever it was, trying desperately to puzzle it out was only going to push it further away from the edges of her consciousness. For now she would concentrate on taking full possession of her new home. Some of the trunks she had brought would need sorting and there was the studio to prepare in the long gallery. Apart from that, Cal had left her a crate of plants and some extra soil to "liven up that courtyard of yours". With all that she doubted that she would get bored any time soon if at all.

A SOFT LANDING

Rosie's search of the library had again brought up nothing. She had
been on the mezzanine floor by the door when her uncle had entered

and gone straight towards the door of the store cupboard before she had a chance to intercept him. Whatever he was looking for must have been well hidden as it was a while before he emerged again and headed out swiftly. This was unfortunate as she'd liked to have asked him about where to look. She climbed down and having nothing better to do she went over to the store cupboard door. The mechanism was hidden so as not to spoil the wall of books.

After a lot of searching, she finally found the lever that opened the door with a small click. By now Rosie was – despite expectations – hoping to find at least a small chamber, but instead she was merely faced with what was plainly the library's store cupboard. Sheaves of paper set on narrow plain shelves lining the walls. There were several inkwells and writing implements and, slightly hidden in the corner, even stood a small bucket, mop and broom. The floor was covered with a rather scruffy little rug and that was it. She stared at the smooth walls and backed out, slowly closing the door.

It was when she turned, disappointment flooding through her, that she felt again that she was no longer alone. Close by the window stood the tousle-haired boy, arms folded, looking at her with great interest. Before Rosie could speak she suddenly sneezed. When she opened her eyes again the boy had gone. She hadn't even heard him leave.

That evening Rosie pulled out *Mari's Book of Dragons and their Magic* again, hoping that this time she would find something else, but there was no change. Not that she had really expected it but she was an optimistic person and you never knew. After the first few pages, which included that dragon picture, there were a few pages filled with scrawls and squiggles similar to those on the parchment she had found inside the wrapping. The rest of the book's pages appeared to be stuck together somehow. She had examined them carefully several times but, short of slicing open every individual page, there was nothing much she could think of and that somehow didn't feel right. She sighed and pulled out the map again.

Studying it carefully, she noticed that certain areas appeared very clearly drawn while others were smudged, as if someone had rubbed over them washing the lines into one another. Having always enjoyed a puzzle, she tried to see if there was anything they had in common. There were three areas she could identify or not depending on your point of view: the ruin by the sea, the sunken garden beyond the terrace and that walled garden, whose wall she had climbed some weeks ago. Of all those the sunken garden appeared the least affected, its outlines clearest. What she did notice though, was that the wooded area she hadn't yet tried to explore appeared to contain another walled garden. It had felt more positive on the right-hand side. Maybe it was time to have a look. With that decided on, Rosie fell into a deep sleep and did not wake until the early morning light was streaming through her windows.

She was up early and after a quick breakfast of thick buttered bread and tea she dashed out. Today felt full of possibilities. She had also made a pact with herself that if anything funny happened, she would simply sit it out. A swallow flew past her when she reached the meadows. Standing still for a moment she watched them, hunting for insects, before setting off determinedly for that strange path.

She came to the beginning of the wood and – like it had on the left – the path changed slightly. The trees were different though. The left-hand side had felt shady. It had taken her quite a lot of courage to enter, whereas the wood on the right felt friendly, almost inviting. There were aspens planted all along a way back and their rustling sounded soothing and welcoming at the same time, familiar in the same way the swallows' flight earlier had felt. There were a lot of trees ranging from birch to alder and beech, hawthorn and hazel, holly and elder, interspersed with numerous dog roses, their pink blooms showing in the foliage. There were other trees too but Rosie didn't know their names. The undergrowth was a thick carpet of plants, some flowering, some not. Here and there birds and butterflies flitted across and it was full of the sounds and smells of a summer's morning. It was pleasant to walk the path this side.

It ended, like the other one, by the corners of walls she knew to be surrounding a garden. The walls were high and rather smooth. There was no way she could climb them. She set out to look for a door. In most places the wood didn't reach the garden walls. The space where she finally found the door was quite open and there was an old – rather overgrown – track that led to it. This door – more that of a castle entrance with a small rectangular door set into a huge arched one – was locked like the other one had been. Rosie had expected that much. Reaching the back wall of the garden, she saw what she had really been looking for: a huge oak tree whose trunk was wedged into the wall.

A few minutes later, after a lot of scrabbling and climbing efforts, Rosie had finally managed to heave herself into the lower branches of the tree. Her hands were a bit raw, her hair a tangled mess and her clothes had definitely proven to be as well made as the shop had advertised. None of this mattered though as the view of the garden more than made up for everything.

It was huge and, from what she could make out through the branches, well kept. It appeared to be a proper castle garden of the type that could keep a castle's inhabitants fed. Why had her uncle not taken her here? It must need a small army of gardeners to keep it neat. She moved further along the branch of the tree to see more when suddenly there was a crack, a sudden drop and she found herself falling.

Something was poking into the calf of her left leg. She moved gingerly and opened her eyes. The view of the garden from here was definitely better, with neat vegetable patches laid out right in front of her and fruit trees visible towards the back wall. But she also happened to be sitting on a compost heap. This wasn't the most immediate problem though. There were sounds of footsteps, coming from the right-hand side of the garden, getting closer and closer, and there was nowhere obvious to hide. While Rosie was still desperately debating with herself the decision was taken from her by the arrival of the garden's occupant. They stared at each other intently. It was difficult to tell which of them was more shocked or surprised.

12

FRIDOLIN

Rosie blinked incredulously. Standing in front of and observing her with an earnest expression in his large green eyes, was a red dragon. What was more, he looked like the spit of the dragon from *Mari's Book of Dragons and their Magic*. Her head went into a spin and her hand went to her chest and touched the little dragon around her neck. Its presence reassured her. She wasn't afraid, merely extremely confused and decided to wait for the dragon to make the first move.

Fridolin studied the human in front of him. From descriptions he knew that this one must be a girl. He wondered if he would be able to distinguish between the ordinary and the dangerous type. He took in the tangled brown hair, the green eyes flecked with hazel, the plain clothes, the fact that she was neither panicking nor sneering and concluded that she was probably harmless. So he enquired very politely, "Do you often sit on people's compost heaps?"

This might be a good time to explain something very fundamental. There have always been dragons and hopefully always will be. Just like with humans some are mainly good and some are bad, to human eyes that is. Crazed rampages – complete with devouring the population and torching the entire countryside – are extremely rare. They are simply not worth it. Truth be told, there are much tastier things to eat than humans in general and princesses in particular and a huge number of dragon species are vegetarians anyway. This dragon, whose name was Fridolin, belonged to a species of gardening dragons and they were very good at it – gardening and vegetarianism, that is.

He had come down from the craggy mountains some weeks ago, following what in his circles was known as a 'garden's call'. He had woken up one day and simply known where he had to go. The reasons for this are as mysterious as those of migrating birds but make perfect sense to those very few learned in dragon lore. In the last decades though, this draw had been virtually non-existent.

The reasons for this were complex but the simple version, told to Fridolin at bedtime, was this: Many years ago his kin had lived in an area surrounded by gardens but had been unjustly driven out. The local princess had complained about them hanging out in her gardens and claimed that they had trampled on her mother's roses. This was complete nonsense, of course, and the princess knew that. It had been she herself who had flattened the garden's most stunning rosebush – about to be entered into a flower competition the next day – by landing on it on her return from a night out. The problem was that her parents were not to know about that night out as they had expressly forbidden her to go. The princess had therefore been a bit at a loss to explain the damage to the rosebush and had swiftly blamed it on the dragons. She had never liked them anyway so she didn't even feel guilty about blaming them.

The King and Queen, who indulged their only daughter, had given the necessary orders. So consequently the whole clan of dragons, who had lived peacefully in the castle's grounds and its surroundings for as long as anyone could remember, had been told to pack up and go live elsewhere.

"Or else...!" the King had said in a threatening tone, pointing to his knights in armour. Now dragons and knights, particularly the ones who carry heavy and very keen swords, don't go together. Everyone knows that and so the dragons had moved far away and into the mountains. Fridolin had hatched there, from a red egg speckled with green, and he was told bedtime stories featuring beautiful gardens, innocent dragons and cruel and manipulative princesses.

All through these musings Rosie had been studying the dragon. She was surprised by his height and stature. She reckoned that he was not much taller than she was. His arrival hadn't been laboured but – in human terms – he had a comfortable girth and beautiful, smooth red scales. His eyes felt so familiar and his face so friendly that Rosie couldn't help giving him a shy smile. To her delight it was returned, albeit a little guarded. Now what?

"The branch broke," Rosie brought out at last, gesturing vaguely to somewhere above her, all the while thinking how bizarre this was.

"Oh," was the only response before they fell silent again. The world was slowly adjusting itself and Rosie suddenly became aware that her bottom was beginning to feel rather damp from the compost heap she was sitting on.

13

Nymphette

QUESTIONS AND PUZZLES BUT NO REAL ANSWERS

It was way past lunchtime when Mrs Baird came across Rosie tucking into a large slice of pie. She could not remember having seen the girl eat with quite so much gusto. Her hair was untidy, her clothes showed signs of a day spent outdoors and despite the clean hands, which she appeared to have washed before taking her food to the table, her master's charge had a definite air of grubbiness about her. Her eyes when she looked up though, were bright and shining with happiness. It was hard to believe that this was the same child, who had looked as if she would rather hide away on her arrival less than three months ago.

Rosie smiled and carried on eating, finally washing down the last crumbs with some herbal tea poured from the jug. She was in the process of tidying up when the sound of thunder rent the air. Before the noise had fully stopped echoing around the grounds, the sky – already foreboding – opened its floodgates and it started to rain in heavy drops. It turned so dark inside that Rosie thought some light would be useful to guide her upstairs. Outside it was so miserable that she simply accepted Mrs Baird's suggestion that she have an early bath. There was no way she'd be going out again that day.

That evening, clearly exhausted from her day, she had fallen asleep early. King Edmar found her on the sofa in the library, lost to the world of wakefulness and carried her to her room without her even stirring.

That night Rosie dreamt. A veritable flood of images marched through her mind but when she woke, just before dawn, it was only a pair of large green eyes that she was able to recall clearly. It was this memory that made her suddenly feel wide awake. She couldn't remember getting into bed last night but she had a distinct memory of what she had done in the morning. She also knew what had afterwards been planned for today. Swiftly pushing her covers aside, she got up and went to the window. Yesterday's thunderstorm appeared to have cleared the air completely and it looked to be a promising day.

Breakfast that morning was a bit trickier than usual. Her uncle was there and Rosie's mind raced along. Should she tell him about the dragon in the garden? What if he didn't believe her? Or worse what if he wanted him gone? Rosie was so busy debating what to do and occasionally wondering if she really had spent hours gardening with a dragon called Fridolin yesterday, that she didn't even realise that her uncle was scrutinising her carefully.

Cup in hand, he was taking in the restlessness and nervous energy of someone with a secret. His niece's face seemed to glow and she seemed completely undecided whether or not she wanted to spill. He made a mental note to keep a closer eye on her and her moods. For now though, nothing about her gave him the impression that she shouldn't just continue to run wild like she had started to in the last weeks. His

Aunt Eleanor had always insisted that children needed space and it was his impression that Rosie had had precious little of that. And anyway, he had business to attend to; business and developments which were slowly beginning to fill him with dread.

As soon as breakfast was finished and she had been excused, Rosie tore off into the grounds. She avoided the sunken garden and went past the huge cedar at the bottom of the lawn without even noticing the boy, leaning against the rugged bark with his arms folded across his chest, watching her intently.

She slowed down when she reached the path's border and made her way through the small wood and to the left-hand corner of the garden. There, hidden by a free-flowering carpet of growth, was a small wooden door. She turned the round knob and heard it lift the latch on the other side. A push later and it had opened, admitting her into the corner of the garden close to a lean-to structure on the left and a small stone cottage hugging the wall further down. Closing the door carefully behind her, she entered the garden looking for Fridolin.

The ground was wet. The flowers and foliage were glistening from the rain. Here and there the sunlight fractured a droplet of water, making it glow like a delicate jewel. She found Fridolin in the greenhouse, right next to the cottage, potting seedlings and joined him after a brief "Morning". For a while they just worked companionably side by side. Like the day before it was so easy to fall into a rhythm. They went through the seedling trays without the need to say much.

That had been one of the most astounding discoveries the day before: they were able to understand each other. Not with signing, gesturing or miming but simply by talking. It hadn't been any different than talking to anyone up at the castle or indeed any person she knew – well, apart from her mother but their communicative problems had nothing to do with the language they spoke.

The other discovery had been that Fridolin didn't seem to mind company at all. Once they had got her off the compost heap and both over their initial shyness, he had shown her round the garden, telling her about the plants and what he had done already and what still needed doing. The point neither of them had touched upon was how either had got there. That was by the by. As she had promised herself that morning, Rosie had simply taken things in her stride. Having someone to talk to so freely had been completely exhilarating and she wanted that to go on. You could also tell that Fridolin was a gardener through and through. The way he talked about the plants were familiar to her, carefully adjusting something here and there while mercilessly yanking out some weeds encroaching on a plant. It didn't matter to her in the slightest that he was a dragon and technically mythical. It would simply be lovely to have a friend.

Last night's thunderstorm had left its traces on the white beach by Sea View House. The sea had raged against the rock, throwing up plumes of spray from the spouting cave and depositing seaweed and debris on the beach. Several times Lucinda had been woken by thunder and lightning, listening to the wind howl around the house and the rain pattering against the windows. For a brief moment she had got up and stood watching the storm from her window, the waves heaving and the landscape becoming visible in snatches of white light. Once she had even fancied a creature crawl out of the sea and onto the beach but by the next light and crack of thunder only the bare pale sand shone in the light. She had gone back to bed and slept fitfully, haunted by snatches of dreams, which eluded her as soon as she surfaced back into consciousness. She woke to sunshine streaming into her room and an urge to paint.

Hours later she was standing in front of the finished canvas, staring. The painting showed the seascape and islands as seen from the studio in the long gallery at Sea View House that morning. With its islands dotted around and the colours it reminded her of the mural the previous inhabitant of the house had painted on the walls of the café but without the dragon in the sky. What caught her attention now though was the sea spray from the spouting cave. She had not been aware of it while painting, but was unable to look away from it now: there on the canvas, amidst the white foam, spray and the blue of the sea the shape of a large blue dragon was unmistakably emerging from the whirl of colours. What was so disconcerting about this was that, undeniable as he was present in her painting, Lucinda was absolutely certain, that she had not knowingly put him in there.

14

Nymphette

THE TIDAL ISLAND

Sitting on the bench outside Fridolin's cottage, with her face turned up to the sun and her eyes closed, Rosie could sometimes still not quite believe what a strange turn her life had taken in the last months. When she was packed off to her uncle's she had had no expectations. There hadn't been any room for thought for a long time. When it had finally been decided what would happen with her, she had already been way too numb to care. Missing her father dreadfully and clinging to Sir Redhill for dear life she had long stopped taking an interest in what was going on around her.

It was this castle somehow, with its strange cutlery, reticent occupants and the friendly feeling of being lived in, that had lured her out. It had helped that her room was comfortable and – most importantly –

hers. She had never really inhabited a room the way she did that one. It almost felt as if it had accepted her as its occupant and was keeping her from harm's way. This was silly of course, but it was the only way she had to describe what her father had sometimes referred to as a sanctuary. No one here disturbed her things or challenged her possessing certain items. Her little plant pots were left in place, where she had put them, and no one had even questioned her about them. Her uncle, whom she saw more rarely these days, didn't pry but he didn't act as if he was bored with her either. It was more, she felt, that they were alike, neither of them great talkers in their way.

It was different with Fridolin though. Fridolin simply loved to talk. Not so much when they were working but quite often when they were taking a break. Over the last few weeks Rosie had learnt about his family along with his parents' travels, his grandparents' retirement valley, his uncle's longing for the gardens of old and his great-aunt Grismelda's endless knitting. He had also told her a great many dragon stories, which quite frequently featured brutal fight-picking knights and malicious and conniving princesses.

The latter always made Rosie feel a little uneasy as, technically – though 'not by behaviour' as her mother would say – she herself was a princess. Never though could she be like one of those nasty specimens in Fridolin's stories! Until she met him it had never really occurred to her that – where they had monsters for valiant knights to fight – the dragons might have unpleasant humans, who had to be defeated to carry the day. In most stories though, they weren't. Despite the pervading melancholy it was still a fascinatingly different way to look at things. There was the story of the stolen egg where a golden egg, which the princess is trying to add to her collection of pretty things, nearly killing the hatchling in the process, gets saved and the princess catches the dragon shingles, which disfigure her beauty but the dragon doesn't come off completely unharmed either. The best ending dragon stories seemed to achieve was balance and Rosie frequently found herself hankering after a human-style fairy tale happy ending – for the dragons of course.

She heard the door creak and Fridolin approached with a tray of